ORCHARD BOOKS
96 Leonard Street, London EC2A 4RH
Orchard Books Australia
14 Mars Road, Lane Cove, NSW 2066
Text © Margaret Mayo 1992
Illustrations © Penny Dann 1992
First published in Great Britain in 1992
This edition published in 1997
The right of Margaret Mayo to be identified as the Author
and Penny Dann as the Illustrator of this Work has been
asserted by them in accordance with the
Copyright, Designs and Patents Act, 1988.
A CIP catalogue record for this book is available
from the British Library.
1 86039 572 4
Printed in Belgium

Little Mouse
Twitchy Whiskers

Margaret Mayo
Illustrated by Penny Dann

• little • orchard •

One day a little mouse called Twitchy Whiskers was running through the woods when she saw an old cardboard box. She stopped and twitched her whiskers and said:

"What's this – a warm house?
It looks just right for one mouse!"

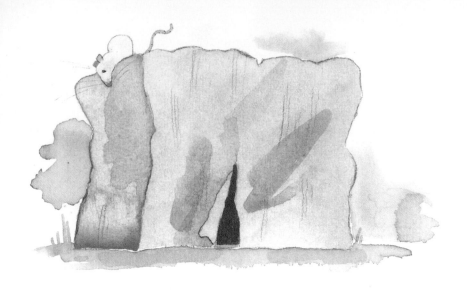

Then she snuffled all
around the box and
twitched her whiskers again
and called out:
   "Who lives in this house?"

Who lives
in this house?

But no one answered. So she crept inside.

After a while a frog came by, and when he saw the box, he called out: "Who lives in this house?"

"Twitchy Whiskers lives here," said the little mouse. "And who are you?"

"I am the Croaking Frog," he said.
"Please let me in."

"Come in," said Twitchy Whiskers.
"Now we are two."

And the frog hopped inside.

After a while a rabbit came
by, and when he saw the box,
he called out:
   "Who lives in this house?"

Who lives in this house?

"Twitchy Whiskers and the Croaking Frog live
here," said the little mouse. "And who are you?"
   "I am the Jumping Rabbit," he said.
"Please let me in."

"Come in," said Twitchy Whiskers.
"Now we are three."
And the rabbit jumped inside.

After a while a hen came by, and
when she saw the box, she called out:
"Who lives in this house?"

"Twitchy Whiskers and the Croaking Frog and the Jumping Rabbit live here," said the little mouse. "And who are you?"

"I am the Clucking Hen," she said. "Please let me in."

"Come in," said Twitchy Whiskers. "Now we are four."

And the hen bustled inside.

After a while a duck came by, and
when she saw the box, she called out:
"Who lives in this house?"

"Twitchy Whiskers and the Croaking Frog and the Jumping Rabbit and the Clucking Hen live here," said the little mouse. "And who are you?"

"I am the Waddling Duck," she said. "Please let me in."

"Come in," said Twitchy Whiskers.
"Now we are five."
And the duck waddled inside.

There wasn't much room.

But they curled up small

and squeezed up tight

and somehow everyone fitted in.

Then a bear came by, and when he
saw the box, he called out:
"Who lives in this house?"

"Twitchy Whiskers and the Croaking Frog and the Jumping Rabbit and the Clucking Hen and the Waddling Duck live here," said the little mouse. "And who are you?"

The bear said, "I am Bear Big-and-Fat who can squash you all flat, so LET ME IN!"

"I am sorry," said Twitchy Whiskers.
"But the house is full. We are curled
up small and squeezed up tight and
the house is stretched to bursting.
So we cannot let you in."

The bear growled,
loud as he could:
  "Rumbling thunder!
I'll tumble
you under!
This Bear
Big-and-Fat will
SQUASH YOU
ALL FLAT!"

Then Twitchy Whiskers and the frog
and the rabbit and the hen and the duck
opened their eyes very wide,
and they saw that
bear coming

down ...

down ...

down ...

right on top of their house. So out
they tumbled and off they ran,
this way and that way.

And the bear sat down on the house *whumpf!* and he squashed it all flat.

But he did *not* squash Twitchy Whiskers
and the Croaking Frog and the Jumping Rabbit
and the Clucking Hen and the Waddling Duck.
He did *not* squash them flat.

They all got back to their own homes,

safe and sound.